For Fia and Rania, new friends.—R.d.S.

For Juliann Margaret—and for those I love.—P.Z.

Text copyright © 2018 by Randall de Sève
Illustrations copyright © 2018 by Pamela Zagarenski

hmhco.com

The text and display type were set in Esmeralda Pro.

Library of Congress Cataloging-in-Publication Data
Names: de Sève, Randall, author. | Zagarenski, Pamela, illustrator.
Title: Zola's elephant / Randall de Sève ; illustrated by Pamela Zagarenski.
Description: Boston ; New York : Houghton Mifflin Harcourt, [2018] |
Summary: A little girl hesitates to initiate a friendship with her new neighbor Zola because she imagines Zola is busy with another friend—an elephant.
Identifiers: LCCN 2017061519 | ISBN 9781328886293 (hardback)
Subjects: | CYAC: Friendship—Fiction. | Neighbors—Fiction. |
Imagination—Fiction. | Elephants—Fiction. | BISAC: JUVENILE FICTION / Social Issues / Friendship. | JUVENILE FICTION / Imagination & Play. | JUVENILE FICTION / Animals / Elephants.
Classification: LCC PZ7.D4504 Zo 2018 | DDC [E]—dc23
LC record available at https://lccn.loc.gov/2017061519

Manufactured in China
SCP 10 9 8 7 6 5 4 3 2 1
4500715693

Zola's Elephant

Randall de Sève

Illustrated by Pamela Zagarenski

HOUGHTON MIFFLIN HARCOURT
Boston New York

There's a new girl next door.
Her name is Zola.
I know because our mothers met this morning
and decided we should be friends.

But Zola already has a friend.
I know because I saw the big box.

begin
F
G
A
D
E
C
B
dreams
HEAVY
FRAGILE
imagine
BELIEVE
STARS
MAGIC
ENORMOUS
elephant
ELEPHANT
friends

You need a big box to move your elephant.

You also need to feed your elephant as soon as it arrives.
(Elephants get *very* hungry.)
I know Zola's feeding her elephant now
because I smell toast.
Lots of toast.

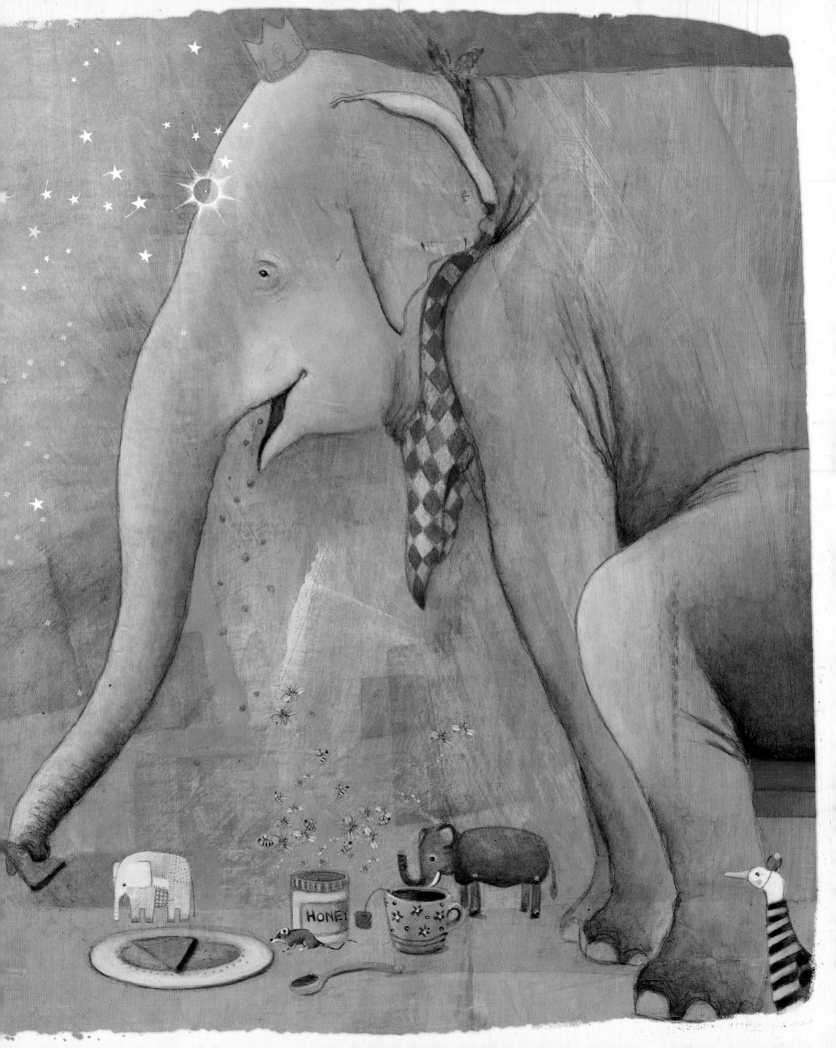

I can't go make friends with Zola now
because she and her elephant are taking a bath.
I know because I hear bath water running
and elephants *love* taking baths.

Elephants also love hide-and-seek.
That's what Zola and her elephant are playing now.
I know because I hear thumping and yelling,
and there's always thumping and yelling
when you play hide-and-seek
with your elephant.

FRAGILE

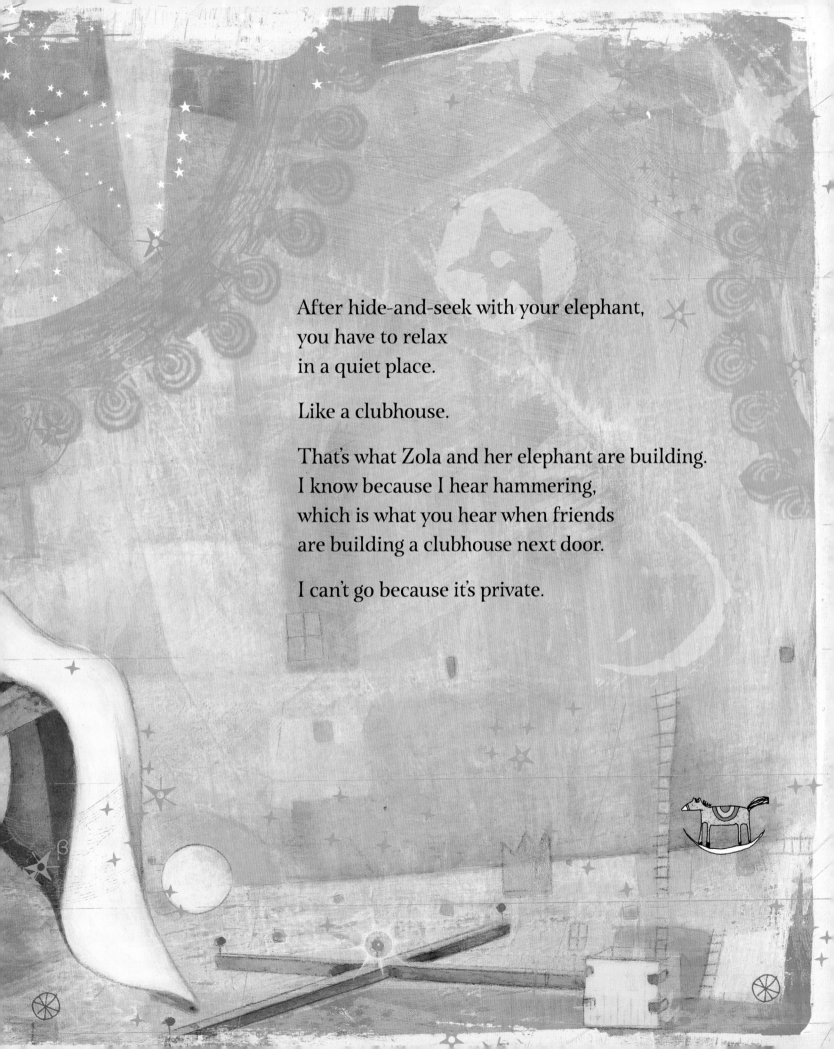

After hide-and-seek with your elephant,
you have to relax
in a quiet place.

Like a clubhouse.

That's what Zola and her elephant are building.
I know because I hear hammering,
which is what you hear when friends
are building a clubhouse next door.

I can't go because it's private.

I'm sure Zola and her elephant
are making their clubhouse very cozy
with pillows
and curtains
and a carpet of stars.

Perfect for relaxing.

Perfect for sharing secrets.

Perfect for sharing stories.

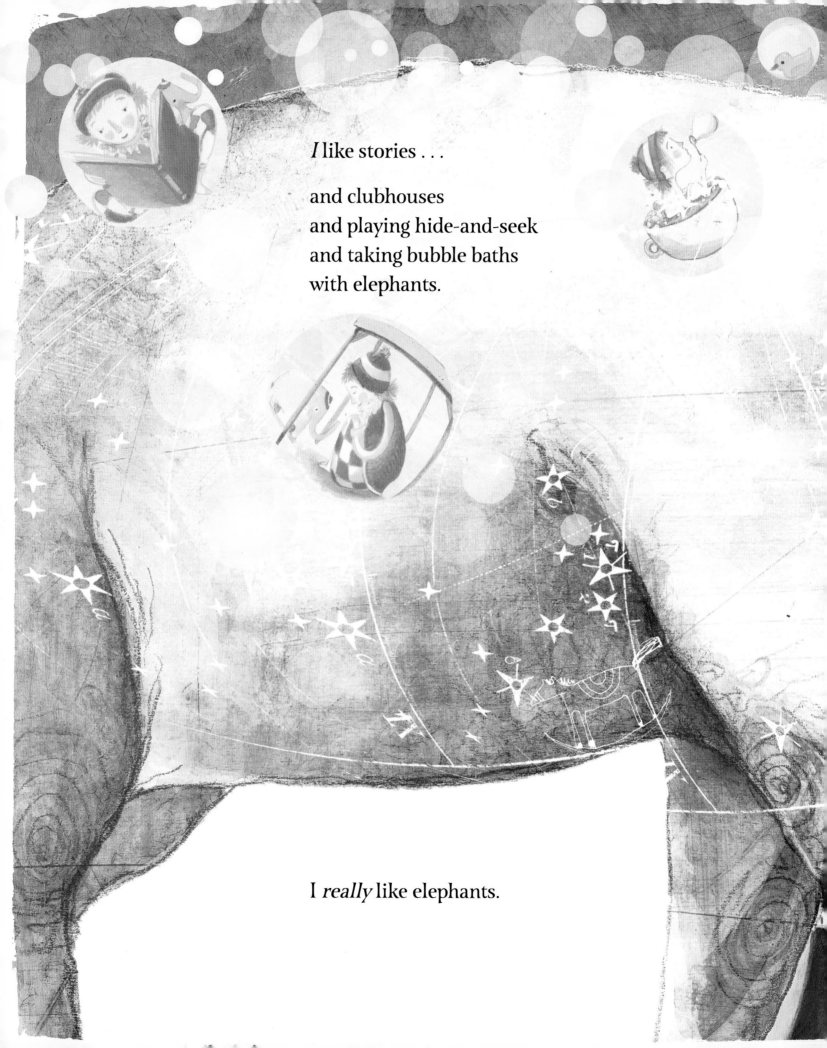

I like stories . . .

and clubhouses
and playing hide-and-seek
and taking bubble baths
with elephants.

I *really* like elephants.

Okay, so maybe Zola doesn't have an elephant.
But do you know what she does have?

A new friend.